ONYX &
BEYOND

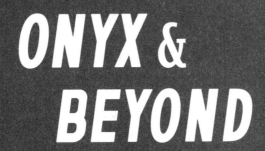

ONYX &
BEYOND

AMBER McBRIDE

INSPIRED BY MARIO McBRIDE

Feiwel and Friends
New York

A FEIWEL AND FRIENDS BOOK
An imprint of Macmillan Publishing Group, LLC
120 Broadway, New York, NY 10271 • mackids.com

Our books may be purchased in bulk for promotional,
educational, or business use. Please contact your local bookseller
or the Macmillan Corporate and Premium Sales Department at
(800) 221-7945 ext. 5442 or by email at
MacmillanSpecialMarkets@macmillan.com.

Library of Congress Control Number: 2024012730

First edition, 2024
Book design by Michelle McMillian
Images on part openers used under license from Shutterstock

Feiwel and Friends logo designed by Filomena Tuosto
Printed in the United States of America by
Lakeside Book Company, Harrisonburg, Virginia

ISBN 978-1-250-90878-0

1 3 5 7 9 10 8 6 4 2

For Bernardine McBride,

all the Moonstones for you . . .

You might as well answer the door, my child,
the truth is furiously knocking.
—LUCILLE CLIFTON

Black love is Black wealth.
—NIKKI GIOVANNI

NEW MOON
1968

Onyx is a rock & so is the moon (kinda).
My gran taught me all about the moon
& how it magics through 8 phases
then rewinds like a fancy cassette tape.

My name is Onyx, nickname X
& 'cause of Gran
& 'cause the moon is a rock
(kinda) like my name,
I watch the sky real closely.
For phases. For magic. For signs.

My favorite phase is the new moon.
It's like a trick play in street football
'cause the new moon is invisible.
It hasn't been blown into a giant lemon.

New moon is there clear as day,
but no one sees.
Kinda like hope or love or invisible wings.

MAMA & GRAN & ME

April 5, 1968

Mama & Gran & me are usually never in a hurry
'cause Mama don't mind being a little bit late to everything
& I have to whisper goodbye to each of my 25 rocks.
    Obsidian & Moonstone are my favorites.

My collection started a while back.
I skinned my knee into a strawberry
while learning to ride my bike
& an older kid named Robin Gibson
gifted me a tiny chunk of Obsidian
as dark as the pavement for luck.
    Robin said, *That rock*
came from a volcano.
Which feels kinda far away.
Like visiting the moon far away.

Sometimes I wish I had an actual chunk
of the moon 'cause I think it would be like
holding outer space in my palm.

. . .

Gran gifted me my wand of Selenite
2 years ago, when I was 8
& said, *This one's gonna cleanse*
    all the others.

Mama gifted me Jade
a year ago & said,
    This one is gonna drench
    you in luck.

Mama & Gran & me are always late
'cause of me. I say goodbye to Jade, Tiger's Eye,
    Bloodstone & Jasper
lined up like colorful candy
on my windowsill.

I keep Rose Quartz on my nightstand
    next to my bag stuffed with marbles.
Rose Quartz is for love.

Mama & Gran say,
There ain't enough love in this world.

I carry Rose Quartz
'cause I want to spread
some of my love,
a little X-tra love
with every step I take.

. . .

My mama tells me,
Onyx, my love for you is like magic.

I think love
can create
magic.

TODAY WE (MAMA & ME) RUSH

April 5, 1968

Today is different.
We move fast
like comets through space.

Gran is out getting groceries
& even though Mama & me
are not supposed to go
anywhere without Gran . . .
    we do.

Mama grabs my hand,
hurries out the door
& tugs me to the car whispering
  over & over again,
    We can't stay still, Onyx.
    The world is burnin' up!

Mama drives like a flash of lightning
the 8 miles from Del Ray
in Alexandria, Virginia,

to Washington, DC, the capital
of the entire United States.

Mama's knuckles crack
& ticktock seconds on the steering wheel
& I think about how bones are not a type of stone
      but *feel* like they ought to be.

DC BURNING

April 5. 1968

In our car we follow the same route the #9 bus takes
& the traffic gets thicker the farther into DC we inch.
  Mama says, *I gotta see it for myself.*

My eyes spread wide
& I hold the lucky Jade
in my pocket tightly.

Mama is right. The world is burnin'.
  Right now, the world is about 10 miles across
& everywhere I look there is fire & smoke & officers
            large & angry
                  in dark blue uniforms.

& the world is burnin'
like when you focus black ants
under a magnifying glass
& they catch fire.

People bang in storefront windows
& flames rage in trash cans like giant torches.

. . .

They bang on everything, but they leave the cars
     slowly passing by on the street alone.
It's like we are in a moving living room,
     looking out the car window
     like it's a TV screen—like we are watching the news.

Mama says, *They burnin' the entire city,*
& I am not sure if Mama is mad or glad or just . . .

          Storefronts cracked, fire hissing up yellow
               in dumpsters. It smells like rotten food
                    being BBQed.

My palms sweat as I watch
bricks knocking out windows,
making buildings look like
they are missing teeth.

Smoke everywhere.

Like DC is smoking
     one gigantic bubble gum cig,
like the ones my cousins & I buy
at the corner store that is now
     missing a front tooth.

HEARD ON THE RADIO

April 5, 1968

Mama twists up the staticky radio
    that sounds the same as the fire
crackling around us.

The radio hollers,
    We must confirm
        that yesterday, April 4th,
            Dr. Martin Luther King
                was shot dead.

& the fires blister brighter
& Mama rolls down the windows
& my eyes sting from smoke
& I wonder if you can be shot but not dead
& I wonder if it's all a big mistake
& I wish I could fly back home
& hide under my bed.

Onyx's Super (Extra) Secret Journal
APRIL 6, 1968

GRIFFIN BOY

My gran calls me her little griffin boy for 2 reasons.
Gran says I am 2 things at once. Fanciful & serious.
Just like the eagle wings of a griffin dream & the lion
    heart is stern.

Second, 'cause of this picture book about a griffin
who swoops down & saves his friends from a flood
on a moonless night using its bright Moonstone eyes
    for light.

I tell Gran, *I ain't like that griffin, though.*
I am all boy, but I've got
giant invisible griffin wings.
        Gran asks,
        Where are your wings?

I say, *Look, look!*
Pointing to my back.
They are right here!

. . .

Gran smiles, tracing
the empty air
behind my back.
I see, they are there,
invisible like the new moon.
But after April 4,
I tell Gran,
I think someone cut
my wings off in my sleep.

Gran nods, wiping my tears.
They'll grow back stronger,
she promises.

WAXING CRESCENT MOON
1970

2 YEARS LATER

Slim
like a thin griffin wing
& also like the thumbnail
of a Black giant that blends in
with the sky.

Waxing like my pops waxes
his car's tires
until I reflect in the rims.

Like when Gran says,
Years wax & wane quickly—
like how Gran grew tired
& flew to heaven.

Like how time flies by so fast
& you can't reverse it.

Like how smoke & fire
from April 5, 1968,
still cloud up my dreams.

I want to fly away
but sink like a helpless stone.
Wingless.

ONYX: 12 YEARS OLD

May 14. 1970

My name is Onyx, like the smooth black stone.
   Or kinda like asphalt—
spit-shined asphalt.

You know,
like if asphalt's mama
took a rag
to its face
& scrubbed
& scrubbed.

Why everybody's
   mama do that?

ONYX THE ASTRONAUT

The word *asphalt* reminds me of the word *ass*,
which is one of those words the barbers
at Dancy's Barbershop spit out but none of us kids say
unless we (look both ways)
          & are alone.

My name is Onyx, but I am not a stone
or (looks both ways)
          ass-phalt.

I am a Black boy racing down Queen Street
    in my cutoff jeans & white T-shirt,
        wearing my PF Flyers, pretending I am an astronaut.
        My backpack is my air pack feeding me life.

I live in Del Ray.
That's a neighborhood
in Alexandria, Virginia.

You know, Alexandria,
like the city of sand in Africa.
Except my city shares a line with Washington, DC.

· · ·

I have a dad, Pops, but he never lived
with Gran & Mama & me.

Pops works at a used bookstore
in DC on 9th Street. I take the #9 bus
every Friday to see him & read
rocket-ship-size piles of books.

Mama used to say, *Your pops & me never loved*
    each other like that, but we both love you
all the way to the moon & back—magic love.

& I would say,
I love y'all back, to the edge
of the known universe & beyond.

THURSDAY CHORES (LAUNDRY)

On Thursdays I get home from Catholic school
& collect all the dirty clothes in the house.

I have to go all the way to the basement to the washing
    machine.
I know how to measure out the detergent. Gran taught me,
before she grew wings & flew to heaven.

I put nickels in the machine & it rumbles
to life like thunder. I watch the clothes spin
in the black hole of the washer.

When they are done, I put them in a basket
& haul them up the stairs to our 3rd-story apartment.

I hang everything up
& open the balcony window
so the clothes can dry faster,
'cause our building ain't fancy.
It doesn't have a drying machine.

They will be dry by the time I get home.

2 PLACES AT ONCE

My pops works at 9th Street Bookstore
& once when I was 9 he showed me the exact line
     where DC & Alexandria meet.
He said, *This is Alexandria & this is DC.*
                    Different laws in each place.

That means *Black folks* are treated different in each.

Sometimes I run down the sidewalk
in my scuffed PF Flyers, knapsack slapping my back
pretending I am an astronaut exploring the moon
& other kids laugh at me as I try to find
the exact line (for Alexandria & DC),
     so I can do magic.
          So I can be in 2 places at once.

If I could be in 2 places at once,
I could live at Pops's & with Mama.
I could be with Gran
     (whose soul is hovering somewhere in the stars)
& I could be here on Earth going to Catholic school.

. . .

My pops's mama is named Emma
& if I could be 2 places at once
I could hang out with my cousins
at Grandma Emma's house & also be with Mama

'cause Mama needs my help much more
now that Gran's body is in the ground & also somehow
sitting somewhere on the dark side of the moon.

Maybe if I could be 2 places at once
I could be the Onyx before April 5, 1968,
(the boy who had an invisible set of griffin wings)
& Onyx now—(the wingless boy).

DARK SIDE OF THE MOON

I've been in Catholic school for 3 years.
Gran enrolled me before she flew away.
She said, *All Armstrongs*
go to Catholic school till the 9th grade.
So, I really didn't have a choice.

Last year at my Catholic school,
the nuns made me play the *night sky*
in the Jesus Christmas play.

The white kids got all the good parts,
'cause the nuns say,
    Jesus don't look like y'all.

But all I wanted to do was be the moon
'cause my name is a stone
(kinda) like the moon.

The nuns said, *It's a shame*
you are as Black as your name.

. . .

Which never made sense to me
because Gran told me,

*Boy, your smile is brighter
than the sun.*

& if I can be the sun,
then for me being the moon
is *X-tra* easy.

THURSDAY CHORES (DINNER)

Spaghetti is easy.
    You just need sauce & noodles.

Before Gran went to the sky
she would make sauce
from juicy tomatoes
& garlic & onions.

I can't do that. That's too much cutting.

I can boil water & put the noodles in
& warm up the jar of sauce in another pan.

I can toast some bread & put butter
& garlic salt on top of it, making
    Onyx's Famous Garlic Bread.

I make the entire box of pasta.
Enough for Mama to warm up
when she gets hungry.

· · ·

I still don't like lighting the gas stove, though.
Reminds me of that day when the city
        was burnin' & Mama & me were driving.

& in my dreams there is still smoke
& fire in trash cans & everything is burnin'.
Even I am burnin' & my skin flakes off
& my magic griffin wings wilt off
like chunks of asphalt from potholes.

Or like the parts of a rocket that
fall, like crumpled litter,
to the ground during takeoff.

I put a note on the leftover spaghetti—
Onyx's Famous Spaghetti, for Mama.

COOL THING ABOUT SPACE #1

Did you know if you light a match in space,
it is much dimmer?

It is *not* easy to burn up space.

X: 12 YEARS OLD (1970)

My nickname is X
'cause nobody is ever
going to call me by my full name.

My nickname is X
like that tall guy with red hair, Malcolm X,
who everyone says is militant.
That's why he got killed,
but I just think his voice was 2 things at once—
 thunder & silence: magic.
I think his voice confused some people.

I also think because he had rusty-red hair
he was like a match on fire & he burned out
 really, really fast.

Thankfully, my hair is black,
like floating smoke that comes after fire.
 I think it means
I have got to watch over things
after fire is gone.

• • •

I think it means I must fly
high above the fire, keeping watch
    & smoke signaling a warning,
but like I said, my wings are missing.

THURSDAY CHORES (RAID MAMA'S CLOSET)

Mama doesn't use all her clothes anymore,
so when she is sleeping, I sneak into her room
& find her most glittery dress.

Mama sleeps a lot, sometimes during the daytime.
I watch her chest rise & fall, steady like a song.
I leave a note on the nightstand—
    Love you to the edge
of the known universe & beyond!

I know most mamas don't sleep during the day,
but ever since the fires & Gran went to the sky,
Mama sometimes mixes up her days & nights.
    Mama sometimes forgets months.

I close Mama's door gently
& I hide the glittery dress
under my bed as part of my super-secret
              build-new-wings plan
& I get ready for bed.

MY OTHER NAMES

My name is Honey, too.
That's what Gran (once)
called me before she started
living in the sky with the moon
& the clouds & the ancestors
one year after the city was on fire.

Gran is not really living in the sky,
but Gran always said,
It's ok to tell yourself a story
if it makes you feel better, Onyx.

So, I tell myself that story.

Honey is also what my mama calls me.
Mama once told me my name is Black Boy, too
& that I can't forget that & I can't
make up stories 'cause Danger is real
    with a capital D & if I forget that
    I might go & end up Gone—
    with a capital G.
        Just like Malcolm.

. . .

Just like Martin Luther King,
who got killed 2 years ago
on the night that the city burned
& smoke rose high in the sky.

Everybody is still crying
& huffing & puffing out smoke
'cause the fires are out but
    he is still gone,
        gone,
            gone.

GONE . . . GONE . . . GONE . . .

Mama says, *Being Gone ain't magic, Honey.*

I answer, *But he is all up in our minds*
    & also somewhere in the sky.

Mama don't like when I talk about the sky
or crystals or rocks. But Pops lets me read
    all about how space is light-years across—
so I believe in impossible things
    & black holes & peace & flying;
even though I have never seen a black hole
    & peace seems impossible & my wings are gone.

Mama & Pops never got married or lived together
(I've always ping-ponged from house to house)
so I don't think Mama knows *all*
the stories Pops lets me read.

Gran taught me about crystals (after Robin gifted me one)
& stories & ancestors—stuff her mama taught her.
Before Gran went to the sky she said,
    You gotta dream, Honey. I couldn't dream.

My parents couldn't dream. Your mama is scared to dream.
You gotta be enough dream for all *of us.*

But then she turned to smoke
    & I broke & I can't dream her back.

THURSDAY FINAL CHORE (LOCK ALL DOORS)

In my pj's I work around the clothes drying
like country flags in the living room.

I lock the balcony door
& double-check the front door.

I make sure we are locked up
safe as astronauts in a spaceship,
which is pretty safe, 'cause of how thick
the walls of a spaceship are.

I check on the letter I hid behind the sofa pillow.

The one from social services.
The one that says they are doing
a wellness check on Onyx Armstrong—
                              in 2 weeks.

The reason why I have to fast-forward my plan.

I HAVE A DREAM (AT NIGHT) *

I dream about flying in the sky
& walking on the moon & discovering magic rocks
& figuring out how to travel light-years in one lifetime.

It's hard to understand a light-year, though.
    It's farther than around the block.
        Or across the USA.
            Or to the pyramids.
                Or across the world.

That's where all the magic is at.
    It's hidden all up in space, up in the sky
just like memories are in our minds
& also in our voices & also
hanging in the air.

& when Gran went to space
a year after my world was on fire,
I think she took the magic with her.

I think that's why my griffin wings left me—
    'cause I wasn't her griffin boy anymore.

Onyx's Super (Extra) Secret Journal

(GRAN'S FAVORITE STORY: HER VERSION OF IGBO LANDING)

Gran used to come into my room to tuck me in.
    She whispered stories about growing up
with tall trees hugging her
in the rural South Carolina heat.

But my X-tra-favorite story
was the one about flying Africans.

They were like astronauts exploring the sky
with sturdy wings that they grew themselves.

It went like this:
It was late at night & 75 Black people
took over a ship bent on taking them to America.

They didn't want to go to hell, to this place
where people harmed them.
They wanted to go home,
but they had been lost so long they had forgotten the way,
& then some great monster's hand stopped
    the ship from moving

& they grew wings (right there on the spot) —
    & they flew home to Africa.

I wonder if I could fly up,
    up, up . . . into space.
If I just believed enough.

FIRST
QUARTER
MOON
1970

Our city is not burnin' anymore
even if the smoke lingers.

My cousins say,
Other cities are burnin', though.

People shoutin' & fightin'
& snarlin' because Black & white people
must go to the same schools.

My cousins say,
They were supposed to mix us all up
after that law that said things were separate
& not equal, but they really makin' them now.

On TV, I see people protesting,
getting knocked down by water,
getting hit & kicked.

The world is on fire
& there is so much smoke
& I think we are all wingless.

. . .

There's a revolution on every corner,
but there is no more magic left.
So I don't know.

I don't know what to do
except remember how to fly.

FRIDAY MORNING THOUGHTS

May 15. 1970

The fan cooling my tiny room makes the calendar
above my bed gently tap the wall.

Reminds me of how stars might sound
    when they twinkle in the sky.

Once I told my oldest cousin, John Quinten, JQ for short,
what the slap of my calendar hitting the wall sounded like.
JQ just laughed & said, *Ain't no boy supposed to be thinkin'*
    about stars twinklin' in the sky, X. There's a revolution
    happening.

JQ says, *We gotta protest. I gotta protest for you,*
    for me, for Grandma Emma & your gran in the sky.
We deserve equal rights! Black people have rights
    that need to be met.

See, the things my cousins be thinking about
are things down on the ground—
    like basketballs, equality & T. C. Williams football.

I be thinking about how things in the sky
can fix things on the ground, 'cause Gran said,
    Your ancestors always got the answers.
    Don't you forget that.

My cousin JQ wears pants that are tight
then big at the bottom. He likes to talk about
    football & protesting.
When I think about football, I think of how the arch of it
is like the trajectory of a spaceship taking off.

Things I be thinking about
are in the sky—
    how do birds fly, why is the moon so big,
how do I hover like smoke?
How do astronauts walk in space?

Things like, do rocks in space have special powers?
Can they heal broken things?
Can they bring back magic?
Can they help my mama?
Can I hold the moon?

ONLY CHILD ONYX: DREAMER BOY

Mama didn't have any brothers or sisters
& Gran didn't have any brothers or sisters,
so on Mama's side it is just
Mama, Gran & me.

Now just Mama & me.

My cousins go to public school, though,
& right before Gran went to the sky,
she enrolled me in St. John's Catholic School
because even though schools are not supposed
    to be separate,
we all live in *our parts of town*, so they still are.
Sometimes I wish I could go to the same school
    as my cousins.
Maybe I'd be less alone. Maybe they would help me grow
giant wings that could fly me all the way up to space.

Pops has 4 sisters & 1 brother, Uncle Rob.
Maybe I think different thoughts because I spend
a lot of time alone: I don't have any siblings,
    just lots of cousins—

(one kid for each aunt)
JQ, Bruno, Willy & Carmen.
We get to hang at Grandma Emma's on most weekends.

Gran said, *I want you to have a good education.*
I don't want to worry.
She said it like that 'cause she knew we knew.
Gran had been sick for a long while.

Sometimes I wonder if all that fire a year before
made her want to turn to smoke & float to the sky.
Now even though I am here on Earth with Mama,
I feel heavy. I feel alone.

ALONE

All I ever hear is my own voice
echoing in my own head.

I am alone on the #9 bus to St. John's Catholic School.
      Alone on the trip to the bookstore to see Pops.
Even when I am not alone (like sweeping
    at Dancy's Barbershop
for extra secret money for groceries) or when I am at my
    grandma Emma's
to see my cousins, I still feel it.

I am as alone as the moon.
I am as alone as a stone—
    'cause I gotta keep *big* secrets.

So, maybe on the ground the world is burnin' up
& protesting, but with Gran uppercase Gone,
    it is up to me.

I gotta be like smoke & hover
& keep Mama safe.

I am only 12 years old but
I've been planning for over a year.
I've been collecting sticks, fabric,
stones & hope.

Since Gran went to the sky—
            it's up to me.

I have to hover like smoke.
I have to bring the magic back.
I have to learn how to fly (again).

SHHH . . . THE *BIG* SECRET

Everyone remembers that day
the city was burnin'
as the day after MLK died.

    Not Gran.

      Not me.

I remember it like this:
Mama got lost driving home—it took us 2 hours
          to get back to our apartment
             instead of 30 minutes.
Gran got so scared she almost called the police
(& Gran hated the police).

Mama said, *Onyx, I done misplaced the road signs.*

I imagined road signs getting up
& hopping on tiny metal legs down the street.

I was 10 when the city was burnin'
& even the lady on the radio was cryin'

& Mama was misplacing road signs
& my 10-year-old hands
    rubbed the Jade in my pocket,
        trying to be brave & . . . & . . .
        & now, sometimes, Mama misplaces time.

        Like for her brain, all the batteries
        have been taken out of all the clocks.

MORNING RITUAL: ALONE

I am thinking about my secret plan
    to help Mama that only I know
when I push back my bright blue comforter
    & walk to the bathroom.
I am thinking about my plan even when
    I am thinking 2 things at once.

Thinking 2 things at once like—
Walk to the bathroom: Walking in space.
  Leave a note (for Mama): Get to school on time.
   Wash the dishes that pile up:
   Put marbles & stones in backpack.
   Smile really big for Mama: Do not cry.
    Brush my teeth: Remember Gran said,
    Clear Quartz is a master at healing.
     Get dressed quietly: Don't wake Mama;
     she was up late, again.
      Put clear Quartz under Mama's pillow:
      Get to school.

DEMENTIA

That's what the doctors said
Mama had. Early-onset dementia.

They said maybe put her in a home,
    & Gran said, *My baby ain't going in no home.*

& we worked together & kept it a secret.
Then Gran went to the sky & Mama got worse.

I read in the bookshop that:
    Sudden changes can make dementia accelerate.

Accelerate is what happens when a spaceship
goes into space—faster, faster, faster.
      Until . . .

BOYS DON'T HAVE LOTS OF THOUGHTS

That's what my cousin Carmen says.
   She says, *I gotta think about my hair.*
Gotta worry about my clothes. I gotta worry about hard things.
Like boys & periods & the police.

I say, *We all gotta worry about the police*
   & keep our heads down.

I don't think some things on her list, like boys,
are something to worry so much about.
But I know what periods are. Gran told me,
   They ain't just the things at the end of a sentence.
      They twist & turn & hurt.

My grandma Emma (who is not in the sky) says,
   Now how one boy got so many thoughts
                  bouncing around in one head?

She don't say it mean, though.
She says it while handing me peach cobbler,
   like she is asking me to share a secret.

But I don't. It's my secret.

Well, it used to be Gran's & my secret,
but now it is just mine.

& my favorite neighbor, Mr. TJ, has been watching.
& my favorite neighbor, Mr. TJ, has been worrying.
& now the wellness check is coming
& they might find out 'cause Mama sleeps
during the day & is awake at night.
& she forgets to cook & forgets to wash clothes.

'Cause Mama forgets Gran
& MLK are both
capital G Gone.

I just keep thinking about how to be
    2 places at once.

There for Mama & there for myself.

WHEN MLK GOT KILLED 2 YEARS AGO

Did you know that sometimes you can get shot
    but not die?
That's what we was all hoping.

I was hoping that the gun messed up.

We were all hoping that 2 years ago,
Dr. King was shot & not dead.

I remember Mama drove for a long time
(Gran was still alive then & at the grocery store)
& my eyes were wide as tennis balls & Mama had water
just behind her lashes from the smoke.

Maybe that's why
    she went
                 & took
        so many
wrong turns.

Maybe if I can fan away smoke with my wings,
maybe she will start remembering things.

ALMOST LATE FOR THE BUS (AGAIN)

I check (2 times) to make sure I lock the door.
Sometimes I get down 2 flights of gray stairs,
all the way to the lobby & have to turn around
         & check 1 more time.

    Mr. TJ is on the front stoop leaning
    on the banister. *You gonna be late, X.*

I hop down all 5 stairs.
I won't, I am as fast as light!
I am working on magic,
on being 2 things at once.
     I can move slow like an astronaut on the moon
     & as fast as a shooting star.

I pump my arms running to the bus stop
to catch the #9 bus to Catholic school.

I pass Ms. Florence's patio with the door open
& music is already floating loudly outside.
    I hear, *Darling, you send me . . .*

                 . . .

I turn right & now I have to go uphill
with my heavy backpack (astronaut pack).
I imagine I am in the last lap of the mile
at the Olympics, the revving engines of cars cheer,
  Go, Onyx! You got this, Onyx!

I make it to the stop right as the bus pulls up.
'Cause sometimes when you pretend real hard—
    magic happens.

BUS RIDE TO SCHOOL

I pay & find my seat next to Robin Gibson,
nickname RG. The boy who gifted me Obsidian
& just graduated from high school,
    which means he is extra cool.

RG's mom used to be great friends
with Gran before she went to the sky.

    RG digs into his backpack.
    Mom made muffins yesterday, X.

It's blueberry & I smile really big.
Thanks RG. I take a huge bite.
It's good.

    X, don't talk with your mouth full.
    You gettin' crumbs all over me.

    RG knocks my shoulder.
    How's your mama doing?
    My moms always asks.

I swallow.

She good. Night shift now.

I lie.

RG nods like he believes me & don't.

So, you gonna finish telling me that story, X?

OVERACTIVE IMAGINATION: BUS RIDE

Everybody on my block knows I have an imagination
    that stretches longer than the Nile.
The Nile is a river in Egypt. Here we got the Potomac.

My eyes brighten. *I got a new story.*
One Gran used to tell me.

    Aight, let's hear it, X.
    RG claps
    his hands together.

Gran (who is in the sky) always said, If you are a Believer &
you Believe with a capital B you can make anything happen.
I lift my foot onto the seat to tie the laces of my PF Flyers.
*So, there is a boy named Magic & he is a superhero even
though he is only 12 years old.*

    Why he so young
    saving people?
    RG taps his knee.

It is because there is a really dangerous thing that shoots death
at people. It's called a gun. But the boy can stop bullets.

Now, how he do that?
RG frowns.

He looks at them real hard & guess what they do? They turn
to water. So, he goes around trying to predict when people are
gonna get hurt & he looks at the bullets really hard & they turn
to water. He wasn't old enough to save Dr. King or Mr. Malcolm,
but he's looking out. They call him Smoke*!*

Now wouldn't that be nice—
something that could stop bullets.

Thanks for the story, X.
RG slings his backpack
over his shoulder.
Tell your mom I said hi.

Sometimes I wonder if I looked hard enough
maybe I could really stop bullets, too.

I told that story to Gran (in the sky) once & she said,
Kids shouldn't have to do what adults should be doing.

COOL THING ABOUT SPACE #2

There is no sound in space
    because there is no atmosphere.

It's just silence
    on top of silence.

I live in the city,
    so I dunno if I can imagine
what that sounds like.

LIST OF THINGS I KNOW ON THE BUS RIDE TO CATHOLIC SCHOOL

1. Mama forgets a lot of things.
2. Sometimes I use my allowance to get food.
3. Mama lost her job because she forgot to go in.
4. We use food stamps.
5. We get a special check.
6. When Gran went to the sky, it got worse.
7. My shoes are 2 years old.
8. My stones don't age.
9. Memories get lost in Mama's head.
10. Sometimes I am afraid.
11. Sometimes I am afraid Mama will . . .
12. Sometimes I am afraid Mama will forget me . . .

& OTHER THINGS I KNOW ON THE BUS RIDE TO CATHOLIC SCHOOL

1. Onyx, the crystal, is made of minerals.
2. Onyx, the boy, is made of minerals & bones & blood.
3. Bloodstone is the stone of courage. We all need courage.
4. Courage is when you do something even if you are afraid. We all get afraid.
5. Being afraid is something that eats & eats at you.
6. Eats you till you don't even act like yourself anymore.
7. Eats you until you don't act like a boy; you don't laugh or smile.
8. I think MLK was afraid of dying; he was never smiling in pictures.
9. I think Malcolm X was afraid of dying, too; 'cause everybody got something to miss.
10. Mama is afraid of forgetting.
11. I am afraid.
12. I am afraid I can't remember enough for 2 people.

TWO MORE STOPS LEFT: SECRETS

My gran, who is in the sky, said,
Onyx, your grandpa got put in an institution
    (when he was young)
        because of the same thing. I won't let that happen
         to my daughter.
Imma take care of her right here.

& Gran was good at taking care of Mama.
She didn't mind talking about the same show
10 times & she didn't mind
if Mama forgot her from time to time.

On days when that happened, Gran put on a song
& the song would pull the memories back to Mama,
like magic, until sometimes the songs didn't work.

Before Gran went to the sky, she set up an account
that checks could go to & she signed us up for food stamps.

Gran taught me how to pick out the best vegetables.
She taught me how to cook for myself & Mama.

. . .

Gran said, *She can have her own little world in this apartment.*

At first Gran didn't plan to go to the sky so soon.
    I know because she always said,
Onyx, after college, you gotta take care of your mama.
Then, after April 5, it was like her heart started sinking.
It sank for a year & then she was gone.

I guess magic ran out
or the city burned too bright
or maybe, I guess the ancestors
in the sky had a different plan.

SIDEWALK CRACKS

The bus drops me off & when I walk down
the sidewalk in my PF Flyers
I wish pavement was made of Obsidian.

I wish I could become invisible when I laid
down on the black stone.

I don't walk like a normal 12-year-old boy.
I walk like I am walking through air that is sticky slime.
    Really slow, like that man who landed on the moon.

I walk slow & I don't like
stepping on sidewalk cracks
'cause they remind me of WWI trenches
that we learned about in school where soldiers
had to sit in long holes on the ground
while bullets whizzed over them.

They remind me of graveyards,
which gets me thinking 'bout funerals,
which makes me think of Gran
& I worry, after they lowered her

into the ground, if she kept falling
to the center of the Earth,
which is just a ball of fire.

I start to run & hop quickly
(at the speed of light instead of sticky slime)
avoiding sidewalk cracks.

Sometimes I don't know
what I am running from.

Sometimes I think I am running fast,
so maybe I'll lift off & end up hovering
    in space.

So fast smoke spews off my shoes
like the roadrunner bird in that cartoon.

PRAYING

When I get to school, I drop my backpack off
　　in my first class of the day.
Then we all shuffle like a giant wave
of kids toward the chapel.

We have to pray every morning
in a language I don't understand,
but Gran always said,
　　Catholic & Baptist both love God
　　just in a different way. So, it's ok to pray.

I don't pray to God—
I pray to Gran asking her to find my wings
that fell off & got lost somewhere.

I pray to Gran 'cause she always said,
　　God is love,
& when I think of love
I think of Gran & Mama
& how I love them to the edge
of the known universe
　　& beyond: magic.

I LIKE GEOLOGY

One of my favorite classes is Geology.
I like to know why the Earth is the way it is.

I wish we had a mineralogy class,
    so I could study crystals.

I wish we had a petrology class,
    so I could study rocks.

Mama used to say, *X, you done always liked rocks.*
    You used to pick 'em up when you were young
& carry them around with you.

I find most of my rocks.
Gran & Pops
gifted me the rest
on birthdays & Christmas.

Sometimes I save enough money
from sweeping at the barbershop
that I can buy one at the Hoodoo shop
2 blocks from Grandma Emma's.

Last birthday, Pops gifted me Obsidian,
which I already have, but this one
was carved in the shape of a spaceship.

Last week I was digging by our apartment
& saw something shimmer like one of Mama's
fancy dresses, like a star winking at me.

Gran used to say, *A miracle is something that happens*
even when everything & everybody says it won't.

So I kept digging 'cause I think I found a miracle,
something I've never found before.

I pulled a piece of clear Quartz
as big as my palm from the soil.

Magic: a miracle.

ROSE QUARTZ

Today I am carrying Rose Quartz.
It's the love stone.
It ain't gotta be boy-girl love.
It can be friend love.
Or Mama love.
Or Pops love.
Or Gran love.
Or Grandma love.
Or cousin love.
Or ancestor love.

Today, I just need a little
    X-tra love.

& stones are everywhere
ready to give a little X-tra.

Onyx's Super (Extra) Secret Journal

(GRANDMA EMMA LOVES BIRDS)

Grandma Emma, Pops's mama, is a birdwatcher.
She even has a pair of special binoculars.
   She sits on her front porch
as still as an Obsidian statue
in her lawn chair watching for birds.

She say, *X, you know, I coulda been*
   an ornithologist: I coulda studied birds.

That's something Grandma Emma & I got in common.
   We both like things that can fly high.

Once when I was 8, I told Grandma Emma
I had invisible wings
   & she looked at my back & said,
     I see them. Big & strong.
       Don't misplace those.

I misplaced them.

WAXING
GIBBOUS
MOON
1970

It's when the moon is almost full.
It's thinking about
flash-lighting as bright as it can go.

I am almost ready.
I almost believe my plan
in my bones.

If I believe hard enough
like the Black people
who grew wings
& flew,
if I can just imagine hard enough,
it will work.

SCHOOL DAY (2 WEEKS TILL SUMMER)

It's 2 weeks
 till the end of school
  & 2 weeks until
   the wellness check.

It's hard
 to focus
  on school
   when so many thoughts
    make my thinking hazy.

CATHOLIC SCHOOL

Friday, May 15, 1970

I learned in school that white kids & Black kids
are supposed to go to classes together.
But because schools get all divided up
by where you live, most schools still look separate.

Once on the bus, RG said,
  One day they just going to have to bus kids
  from different districts or things are not going to change.

Two years ago, when I got the scholarship
& started going to Catholic school
everything was already mixed.

Our school looks like
a Dalmatian Stone.
  All speckled.

Which is fine except
at lunch the Black kids
still sit together.

We sit like we live,
    in our little groups
ignoring each other.

Actually, now, everyone ignores me——
especially after Gran went to the sky
& I started talking less, joking less because
I had to keep my big secret
& plan my super-secret plan.

I started getting called Stone Boy.
Which is not that original
considering my name.

It reminds me of Pinocchio.
    He was a wooden boy
& nobody liked him.

I think I am most like Pinocchio——
    brown & lonely & hard like my name.

HISTORY CLASS

History is my second favorite class because
    His-Story makes it sound like it's my story
& even though we never learn about people
    who look like me,
I like knowing about things that happened a long time ago.

Makes me think about time & how long it takes
for a crystal to form in the ground.

& sometimes, I don't really listen all that much in
    His-Story class.
I just think about my story, the story I want to happen.
I want to be the boy who saved his mama,
    the superhero boy
named Smoke, who can stop bullets & fly high in the sky
    & collect all of Mama's memories
    & keep them safe in her head.

Sister Joanna is one of the nuns who is Black
    like me & sometimes when she sees me looking
out the window not paying attention, she taps my desk
    gently twice.

I don't mind. It's better than when the nuns
yell at me, or when they ask me questions
they know I don't know the answers to.

HER-STORY (RUBY)

Sister Joanna points at the chalkboard.
This is Ruby Bridges in 1960. She had to be
escorted by US Marshals to school.

Why they have to mix things up in the first place?
a Black kid in the middle of the class asks.
It's Big Nick. He has been held back twice.
He sounds a lot like my cousin JQ.
My brother said his school is still mostly separate
& he said he don't care, 'cause mixing schools
don't change nothing.
He raises his clenched fist.
Black Power.
    Sister Joanna tries
    to find her words.
    So, you don't want things
    to be equal?

I ain't say that. I said it don't make no difference
if they hate us in the same school or a separate school.
Big Nick taps the desk
with his tiny pencil stub.

. . .

Sister Joanna says,
What do you think, Onyx?

I swallow & everyone is looking at me
like I am a rocket about to take off
& I remember what Gran said.
I want things to be equal,
but kids shouldn't have to do what adults should be doing.

Big Nick slams his desk.
If we don't do nothing, who will?
Grown-ups don't care & everything ain't magic
like in your dreamworld, X!

& I shrug because I think he is wrong.
I think some things are magic
if you believe hard enough.

& Sister Joanna doesn't look mad or sad.
    She just looks at me like she is looking
at the sun too hard. Her eyes tear up.

COOL THING ABOUT SPACE #3

One million Earths
    can squeeze
        inside the sun.

So, if you are feeling sad,
    if you are feeling as small as the Earth
        compared to the sun,
            you are feeling X-tra tiny.

LUNCH LINE

I study my feet in the lunch line,
thinking about how they are so heavy
& it feels impossible for them to hover like a plane.

Lunch is always the same—hamburger or hot dog,
& if I keep my eyes down no one talks to me.

I hold my tray tightly between my hands.

I hear him coming before I see his feet.
    It's Big Nick.
He flips my tray out of my hand.

& my best meal of the day splatters on the floor.

My hands clench into fists
& I grit my teeth.

    What you gonna do about it, X.
    You gonna get grown-ups to help you?
    He's all up in my face.
    You want to be equal?

You want to bow for the white man?
That's not what I said.
I think of the love stone in my pocket.
I think about how it might be broken
because there is no love
in Big Nick's face.

I think how magic might be broken.
How I might be broken.
How Mama might be broken.

    Oh, now I don't know how to hear?
    He bends to see if tears
    are in my amber-colored eyes.
I exhale slowly,
wishing I could fly away
like those people Gran
told me about.
    He dumb
    just like his mama!
Don't talk about my mama.
I glare at Big Nick.
Ever.

    Or what?
    He shoves me.

I don't know who swings first,
but I am swinging,
hitting, kicking.

· · ·

Ain't no one
gonna talk about
my mama,
    I YELL.
       I SCREAM.
          I SHOUT!

My knuckles ache
& I imagine them
hard as Diamond,
hard as the moon,
hard as my name.

COOL THING ABOUT SPACE #4

Sunsets on Mars
    are sad.
        They are actually blue.

WAITING IN THE PRINCIPAL'S OFFICE

Once I asked my pops if there could be a funeral
    & you don't die, just like sometimes
you can get shot & not die.

    He said, *X, now what kind of question is that?*

    I said, *Just wonderin'.*

I was just wondering because I had a dream
about Gran (the one who is in the sky now).

I had a dream about Gran.
I was so lonely I started talking to my shadow.
Made me start wondering if planets get lonely
               light-years apart.

    Big Nick nudges my knee.
    Didn't know you could punch.

I mean mug him.
Don't ever talk about my mama.

. . .

Never again, X.
Big Nick looks at me
almost like he is proud
with a bluish-black ring around his eye.

& I think this is what Big Nick meant.

I am mad at him because he talked
about my mama.

I don't hate him.
    I could never hate him
& why should I want to be around
people who hate me?

THE DREAM I HAD ABOUT GRAN (IN THE SKY)

When Gran went to the sky, it was sudden,
a year after the city was burnin'. I went to school
& when I came home
  Mama said, *Gran has gone to the sky.*

There was a funeral.
The ground was cut open
& closed
& the ground scarred.

& in my head I promised Gran
I'd take care of Mama, I would find a cure
for the incurable thing, I'd magic it.
I'd figure out how to help her memory
that started getting hazy a year before.

But after 6 months, Mama was getting worse
& I was trying to keep our secret,
so Mama could stay at home
& I didn't have a plan.

So I prayed
as hard as I could
to Gran (in the sky)
       & she sent me a dream.

GRAN'S DREAM FOR ME

The dream was as clear as Quartz.
Gran looked younger & she said,
    Onyx, you just gotta fly.
You gotta soar as high up as you can.
Onyx, you gotta be strong like your stones.
Remember, there is a stone for every situation.

I woke up & knew
    Gran wanted me to fly.
She wanted me to fly as high as I could—to the moon,
to find the perfect stone & bring it back to Mama.

Some things you just wake up & know
& I knew she wanted me to fly like those Black people
in her Georgia red clay stories.
    I'd have to believe hard enough
        I'd have to fly.

I'd have to build my own wings.

WAITING IN THE PRINCIPAL'S OFFICE (STILL)

It's not like waiting in a regular principal's office.
    I know because Willy, my cousin, says his principal
is Black & wears jeans on Fridays.

My "principal" is a white man in robes that look like
    Mama's robe except layered over each other 5 times.

He stares at me & Big Nick both sitting on our hands,
    because sometimes the nuns hit our knuckles
with rulers & we don't want to give them any ideas.

    He says, *Do you think Jesus*
    would want us to fight?

Big Nick & me both shake our heads, *No.*
But I think we both mean, *Ain't you the one*
who is supposed to know
what Jesus wants?

Big Nick gets outside detention
(because he gets in trouble all the time).

· · ·

I get inside detention helping Sister Mary Roberts
clean her classroom after school till summer.

Which is a total bummer.
Which is not part of the plan.

AFTER SCHOOL WITH SISTER MARY ROBERTS (DETENTION)

The school calls my house to let Mama know that I'll be an
hour late because of fighting. She answers the phone &
I hope she forgets before I make it back home. Some things I
want her to forget, she don't. But I guess memory is like that.

Sister Mary Roberts's classroom is where I am helping.
The room has 20 rusty desks & her big desk in the front
that has so much rust I think I could write my name in it.
The ceiling has stars hanging down on glittery strings.
It reminds me of shooting stars that are just big pieces of
rock coming into our atmosphere.

Sister Mary Roberts says,
Nice to meet you, Onyx.

I nod.
You can call me X.
That's what everyone calls me.

Like Malcolm X?
Sister Mary Roberts frowns.

. . .

Here's the thing. Sister Mary Roberts is white, so she don't
get how things can be 2 things at once—especially Black
things. Like I can be here helping her & also at home helping
Mama with the notes I leave everywhere. Like, I think Sister
Mary Roberts is rude for frowning about Malcolm X, but she
is also one of the kindest teachers & nuns.

No, just X like the letter.
I shrug with the white lie.

Sister Mary Roberts has really big glasses that remind
me of my pops, but her eyes are gray & look like ghosts
looking through you. I feel like Sister Mary Roberts can see
all my secrets. That she knows about the love rock in my
pocket & how I had to get myself ready for school. Sister
Mary Roberts looks like she knows I stay at my grandma
Emma's, Mama's, or Pops's depending on the day. That
I keep the schedule so no one will suspect about Mama.
They will just think she is working extra hard. Sister Mary
Roberts looks at me like she knows that I am about to learn
how to fly.

Well, X, do you like space?
She points to a map of the solar system.

I dunno.
I lie.

I look at the picture of space & I think those planets are big
rocks that could never fit in my pocket. I wonder if they

are 1 rock all the way through or if they change, like Earth,
going to the center.

Well, you know a man landed
on the moon.

Mama says, *That was in a studio. There ain't no way to get to*
the moon. We all watched & thought that it had to be a trick.
Like in the pictures. Cameras made it look like the moon,
but it couldn't be. I don't think we should be able to go to
the moon & not fix other things, like getting Dr. Martin
Luther King undead & finding out why brains forget things.

Sister Mary Roberts grabs a big book.
Your detention today is to read this.
Don't you want me to clean?
I point to the piles of paper
& the open glue bottles.

Sister Mary Roberts crosses her arms.
Today I'll clean up.
You read.

It's a large book about space & I am thinking 2 things at once
again. I am thinking I am glad Sister Mary Roberts is letting
me read because I don't want to clean up other kids' glue. I am
also steaming inside because Sister Mary Roberts handed me
a book like I had never "read" a book. She handed me a book
like she was handing me the future. She handed me a
book like a white person handing a Black kid a precious stone.

. . .

& I think there are probably things
    that the moon understands
that the sun never will, but I guess
they still work together.

We need them both to live.

PLANNING ON THE #9 BUS RIDE HOME

I've already tried lots of Earth stones under Mama's pillow.
    I even dug up some rock I didn't know
        & washed it in the sink real good.

I thought maybe this rock fell from the moon
a million years ago; maybe this rock will work.

It didn't.

Last week when I was sweeping the bookstore
with my pops, I took a bright yellow stone
that sat on the bookshelves & nested it
under Mama's pillow.

It didn't help.

I asked Pops,
You know how it was impossible
to go to the moon & now we can.
Do you think people
will ever be able to fly?

· · ·

Pops said,

Anything is possible, Onyx.
Look how far Black people have come
in 100 years.

BOOKSTORE ON 9TH STREET, DC

It's Friday, so I take the #9 bus that carves
a straight line right into Washington, DC,
to see Pops at the bookstore.

The buildings huddle closer together
& the roads get bumpier.

I get off on 9th & walk fast,
pretending I am an astronaut in a hurry.

Pops looks cool at the checkout
& Uncle Rob is in the natural history aisle
straightening up the leaning tower of books.

> *My little man,*
> Pops says, smiling.

Hi Pops.
I give him a big hug
'cause Pops is big on hugs.

· · ·

Why your face look long?
Pops says, holding my cheeks
between his hands.

'Cause school was long,
I say.

Pops stands up straight
& frowns.
You hear that?

I hear the subtle *ding*
of the Good Humor
ice cream truck.

Pops runs toward the door
faster than me, saying,
Ice cream fixes everything.

LITTLE MAN

Pops nicknamed me Man
'cause he says I am always
trying to act grown—
    even when I was real young.

He says that once when I was 3
he found me reading the newspaper
upside down, with a mug of water in my hand.

Pops hands me one of those ice creams
with a chocolate shell that cracks
E
V
E
R
Y
W H E R E
    when you bite it.

    How's your mama doing?
    He sits on the stoop beside me.

. . .

She is good,
I say, taking another bite.

   I might stop by & say hi.
   Pops looks out
   at the street
   as he talks.

I try not to jump
out of my skin.
She is real busy.

   Pops looks down at me.
   Glad she has you around,
   little man.

Uncle Rob steps out of the bookstore
onto the stoop. *I gotta go to my other job.*

You got another job,
Uncle Rob?

Yeah, at the natural history museum.

Uncle Rob steps off the stoop & goes down the street
with so much pep in his step it looks like
he might be flying for a millisecond.

ERRANDS AFTER BOOKSTORE

After seeing Pops,
I get off a few stops early,
because we don't have any more milk.
I used it in my Cap'n Crunch.

Gran taught me you should always have
    milk, eggs, peanut butter & bread in the house.

You can't starve with those on hand.

I walk (like a boy in space) to the grocery, trying not to see
every crack as a giant hole ready to devour me.

The store is cool compared to outside
& music plays quietly.

Other kids in the store are in the candy aisle.
    But I don't have time for candy.

I grab the peanut butter & bread first,
because Gran said, *Get the not-cold things first.*
I get the eggs & milk next.

• • •

I make sure they bag
the bread & eggs together.

Then I walk home.
Still alone.

13 DAYS TILL SUMMER

My calendar has a different rock
for each day & facts about it.

Pops got it for me the year I turned 12.

The calendar also has a countdown till
the last day of school.

I've circled May 29, 1970,
in red pen. Today is May 15
& the stone is Moonstone.

Moonstone is not found on the moon.
It is actually found in the ground
all around the world.

In India & Australia
& Mexico & Brazil.

. . .

Moonstones mean—

H
  O
    P
      E.

MAMA USED TO . . .

Sometimes looking at calendars makes me sad,
because I think of Gran (in the sky)
& think about things Mama used to do.

Mama used to wake me up bright & early
    yelling my name loudly
        & the kitchen smelled like bacon & syrup.
Mama & Gran used to make yeast rolls together
& it was my job to watch the rolls rise in the oven
like inflating golden suns.

But I get myself up now
    & I haven't had yeast rolls in a year.

It started about a year ago,
    when Mama switched up night & day.
She woke up when I came home from school
& went to bed right before I woke up.

So, I learned how to set my alarm
    'cause it is easy to forget day & night.

. . .

There is always something in the fridge I can warm up,
   though.
   Mama makes it while she is awake.
Mama says, *I forget a lot, Onyx,*
      but I'll never forget to feed my baby.

So now, in the mornings I say hello to my rocks.
I eat cereal or a waffle without syrup or a plate.
   I pull on some pants & put on my PF Flyers.

I grab the change from the table (for the #9 bus)
& leave a note for Mama that says,
   Good morning from Onyx.

MAMA FORGETS MORE

About 2 weeks ago, Mama stopped leaving notes for me.
    They used to say, *Good morning from Mama.*

For the last 8 days, nothing.

It feels like time is running
too fast & also too slow.

I keep trying to hold time still
like my superhero Smoke,
but it keeps ticking . . .
        ticking . . .
                ticking . . .
So, I actually take the batteries out of all the clocks.

NIGHTTIME SPACE BOOK FROM SISTER MARY ROBERTS

1. A light-year is how long it takes for something to travel at the speed of light for a year (check, knew that).
2. Uranus rotates on its side & also sounds like *your anus*, which is funny (check, knew that).
3. There might be water on other planets (did not know that).
4. If there is water on other planets, that means there could be life?
5. If there is life, there could be medicine?
6. Space holds a lot of secrets. A lot of magic.
7. Things from space are on display in the museum.
8. Maybe the special things in the museum are carrying magic.
9. Maybe the magic in things from space can bring more magic here. On Earth.

THE TOP-SECRET PLAN UNDER MY BED

After my dream about Gran (in the sky)
I remembered a story she told me:
   During the Middle Passage
some Africans, stolen from their homelands,
prayed to the ancestors, jumped out of ships,
grew wings & flew back home to Africa.

When I was little, I asked Gran,
   How did they grow wings?

Gran said, *Because they had to.*
   Sometimes magic happens.

I have to save Mama.
So, I've decided to build wings
that can maybe get me to the moon
because when my ancestors jumped
they didn't have anything.
      No wings. Nothing.

I am building wings because I want to help
my miracle happen. If I build them,
I have to fly.

. . .

Under my bed, I have 6 old shirts
draped over paper towel rolls
in the shape of 2 half hearts—
            in the shape of wings.

I snuck into Mama's closet & took
her dress with purple feathers.
I borrowed colorful feathers
from Gran (in the sky)'s hat.

I've built wings.
My superhero name—
Smoke!
The Black boy with wings.

WHENEVER I THINK OF WINGS (IN BED)

I tuck myself in
thinking about my wings
just underneath my bed.
Which makes me think
of Gran's soul (in the sky)
& Gran's body (in the ground).

On the day of Gran's funeral,
Mama held my hand.

You know what a funeral is?
It's when the soul & body separate.

It's when they dig through dirt
& stones & crystals to lower
a coffin into the soil.

I wonder if Gran can grow wings
in such a small space.

I wonder if the crystals in the soil
remind her of stars.

Onyx's Super (Extra) Secret Journal

(GRANDMA EMMA TAUGHT ME THE HIGHEST-FLYING BIRDS)

1. Rüppell's griffon vulture: is 20 pounds & can soar at 37,000 feet!
2. Crane: is grace-filled & can glide over the Himalayas.
3. Bar-headed goose: can travel 1,000 miles in a day.
4. Alpine chough: builds nests 21,000 feet above the ground.
5. Bearded vulture: eats bones easily.

I tape 5 bird feathers to my wings
& pretend they come from the highest-flying birds
even if they are just from crows & sparrows.
I hope together they will help me soar . . .

FULL MOON

1970

The perfect time for magic.
I open my window
& let the moonlight filter in.

I pull my wings from under my bed
& let the glow drench them
in magic.

SATURDAY PLANNING FOR FLIGHT

I need near picture-perfect conditions to fly.
    Not too windy but not wind-less.

The weatherperson on the radio says
    the day after next will be windy & warm.

The best flying day is Tuesday.

I pick out the best outfit—
    black pants & black T-shirt.
I make sure the belts I use to strap
the wings to me are just right.

Last, I take the sparkly piece of fabric
I borrowed from Mama's closet
& drape it over the tops of the wings.

My wings are strong & made of love
    & I imagine Gran in heaven
        always on my side saying,
          The boy tried, the boy believes,
            give the boy wings!

SATURDAY DINNERTIME

There is a peanut butter sandwich on the counter.

We always got one or the other—
    peanut butter, no jelly.
    Peanut butter & jelly, no bread.
When we don't have bread, Mama puts peanut butter
& jelly on a toasted waffle.

I take a bite of my sandwich before tiptoeing
    to Mama's room.
All the windows are hugged closed
& I hear her steady snores.

I wonder if when Mama is dreaming,
    she remembers everything?
If her dreams are more real than real life?

I pull my space book out of my backpack
& take my sandwich to the balcony.

I sit & read till the sun sets & it's time to sleep.

. . .

I go to bed Saturday night hoping,
praying to Gran & my ancestors to help me fly
until I hear pots banging at 3:00 a.m.

Mama is awake.

3:00 A.M. POTS BANGING

I throw my covers off & tiptoe to the kitchen
where Mama is humming & cooking a meal.
She is heating up frozen corn with hot dogs mixed in.

Hi Mama,
I say softly,
so I don't scare her.

> *Honey, you slept late.*
> She keeps stirring
> her corn & hot dogs.

Mama, it's 3:00 a.m.,
I say, twisting my hands.

Mama stops stirring & paces across the room
to open the window & see the darkness
stretching forever like an endless shadow.

Her brows scrunch together. Her mouth opens a bit,
like she is trying to figure out how the sky can play tricks.
Mama turns to me & smiles real big.

I know, Honey, I just got hungry.
She pulls down 2 bowls.
You hungry?

I could eat,
I say & take a seat.
Mama places a bowl down.

Hope I didn't wake you.
Mama hands me a spoon.

I was already awake.
I lie.

I lie about being hungry, too, because I am not.
I lie about the day of the week, too, because I want Mama
    to smile.

You know, Onyx,
maybe we should go see
Martin Luther King speak.

I swallow a piece of hot dog whole.
Mama, Dr. King is capital G, Gone.

MAMA'S SONG

I tell Mama about school & His-Story
& about how Dr. King is capital G, Gone
& she says, *Oh yes, of course.*

Mama laughs at the jokes I tell her & it feels like
the warmth of summer has arrived early.

But then, Mama has that real distant look on her face.
The look only can be fixed by 1 thing.

I run to get the record & put the needle down—
    Ain't no mountain high enough,
    Ain't no valley low . . . ,
I sing, smiling at Mama.

    Mama points at me.
    To keep me from getting to you,
    Mama sings (from memory).

. . .

& we dance & sing at 3:00 a.m.
'Cause for Mama, it's 12:00 noon
& I took all the batteries
out of all the clocks
so anytime is a good time
to remember to dance.

SUNDAY MORNING WALK

Mama doesn't remember Sundays,
so we don't go to church.
    I don't think people notice 'cause Gran
    really was the one who took me to church.

That was until last week when
a social worker came to check on me
& I told them Mama was working
& they said they would be back
    on May 28.
Which was bad 'cause I thought
I'd have the entire summer to learn
how to fly.

Later I found out that
one of the church ladies had said,
He ain't been to church in almost 6 months
& I always see the boy by himself.

I put on my shoes to go on my Sunday walk.
Today, I walk real slow like a man in space.
I walk & walk & walk until I hear someone call my name.

. . .

I look down an alleyway & RG is there with some chalk.
I run down the alley to see what he wants.

   Look what I drew,
   he says with his hands
   on his hips, admiring his work.

On the brick wall are 2 wings
with swirls of colors in the middle.

   Go ahead stand there,
   RG says. *Now it looks
   like you went & grew wings.*

I grew wings,
I whisper.
It's a sign.

MONDAY AGAIN

May 18. 1968

There are a lot of rules in Catholic school that don't make sense.

1. DON'T ask why Jesus is white.
2. DON'T ask why Jesus has blond hair.
3. DON'T ask how 1 man parts a sea with a staff.
4. DON'T ask why God would want someone to kill his son.
5. DON'T question Scripture.
6. DON'T ask why no one looks like you.
7. DON'T question why sometimes people get sick.
8. DON'T question if miracles happen for normal people.
9. DON'T FLY.
10. DON'T . . .

IF I (ACTUALLY) WENT TO CONFESSION

1. It's a secret, but my mama don't remember things.
2. It started 2 years ago & I help keep it a secret.
3. I heard that people who forget are put into hospitals.
4. I heard that people who forget sometimes are called crazy.
5. My mama ain't crazy. She remembers me.
6. My mama remembers my favorite food.
7. My mama remembers important things: like love & hope.
8. Sometimes my mama forgets she never got married.
9. Sometimes I gotta tell her & she cries real hard like she failed at something.
10. If there is a God & a Jesus, why they let things like this happen?
11. I am afraid that one day Mama will forget me.

CONFESSION: ROCKS I LIKE MORE THAN GOD

I handle my rocks like miracles.
I check my wings because tomorrow is flying day.

1. Clear Quartz: Gran says, *This is the stone all
   rootworkers have.*
2. Black Tourmaline: Gran gave me one after I broke
   my arm that one time. She said it would get those old
   scared feelings to go.
3. Amethyst: I used to have nightmares. Mama put it
   under my pillow.
4. Agate: Gran gave me this one right before she died.
5. Obsidian: I keep holding on to it. It's supposed to help
   with the truth.

Sometimes I think I should tell the truth about Mama.

MONDAY BUS RIDE TO SCHOOL

I made sure there was food in the fridge for Mama
& on the bus I open the book across my lap
'cause I don't see RG on the bus.

The very last page says that a lot of the information
about space is from the natural history museum.

It says the museum is in DC, which shares a line
  with Alexandria.

I think of my wings flapping
as the bus bumps up & down
& I think it must be rough
to take off into space.

It must be scary for a moment,
but then you blast through
the atmosphere like magic.

I think the sky must capital L, Love,
to help it soar like that: magic.

SCHOOL DAY (11 DAYS TILL SUMMER)

I stand outside the lunchroom for what feels like 10 light-
years with my lunch in my hands. My hands are darker than
the brown bag & I remember how Gran once said, *People
sometimes didn't like your mama because she was darker than
this bag.* It's strange to me that things that are dark are bad.
Black hole.
Blackout.
Black death.
Black cat.
Blacklisted.
I am making a list in my head when Sister Mary Roberts
taps my shoulder & invites me to her room to eat lunch.
I still have her space book under my arm & I nod yes. It
hasn't always been like this. I used to be one of the kids that
could talk with everyone. I used to be able to morph like
matter into different shapes.
Dr. Martin Luther King.
Marcus Garvey.
John Lewis.
Malcolm X.
Onyx (me).
I sit down at the rusty desk that my knees have trouble

fitting into now. I am just noticing that in the year since Gran died, I've gotten tall. Gran used to mark my height each year on the wall in the apartment. Like a new chapter in a book. Sometimes, I am not sure if I made the jump to 12 because we did not mark it. Mama started forgetting more without Gran helping & then my birthday slipped away.

1 X-tra inch.

3 X-tra inches.

4 X-tra inches.

I take a small bite of my waffle sandwich & I think Sister Mary Roberts is saying something important to me but I feel like I have fallen into a black hole.

PERMISSION SLIP

Onyx, I was asking
if you liked the book?
Sister Mary Roberts frowns.
I shake my head & focus
on the classroom around me.

I pull myself out of the comforting
darkness into the messy light.

I like it a lot,
I say.

Have you been
to the natural history museum?
She taps her pencil.

No.
I move my legs
& they slam against
the top of the desk.

My class is going this week.

Maybe you can join us.
She stands & grabs
a piece of paper.

I take it.
Permission slip?

Yes, if you get it signed,
I'll pull some strings.
She whispers,
They have some artifacts
from the book on special
display from NASA.

The edge of my lip pulls
into a smile.

I have a backup plan for if my wings don't work.

MONDAY AFTER SCHOOL: HELP FROM COUSINS

Today, I go to the barbershop,
then Grandma Emma's house
& tomorrow morning, I'll sneak home
to test my wings.

But first, I meet my cousins
on our corner
to ask them for a big favor.

JQ, Willy & Bruno
high-five me.
Carmen gives me
a quick side hug.

Our corner is the center
of our universe.
It is only a block away
from all of our bus stops.

*I need some help
moving something,*
I say, kicking the sidewalk.

With what,
Willy says, crossing his arms.
It's getting hot out.
It's just something important.
I try not to look them in the eyes.

Carmen fans herself.
I ain't helping with nothing
if you don't tell me what it's for.
I gotta move some mattresses
from the dumpster to the alley.
Carmen stops.
Lord, y'all still jump off
the second floor?
For fun?
Yea. I half lie.
& there are good mattresses
at the dumpster today.

We better hurry.
JQ starts walking.
Or Grandma Emma will ask questions!

OLD MATTRESSES

When JQ was 12 & I was 8, we used to move mattresses
under apartment windows & jump like wingless birds. We
used to pretend that we could fly. Carmen watched from
the bottom & made sure the mattress was in the right place.

I figure if I am going to try to use my wings, I should have
a safety net.

It only takes us 10 minutes to get to my street. The
mattresses are still at the dumpster. JQ & I tug one toward
the alley that separates 2 of the apartment buildings. Bruno
& Willy tug the other one around to the side. We stack
them on top of each other like a giant mattress cake.
   This is a good spot,
   but don't go higher
   than the second floor,
   Bruno says,
   dusting off his hands.

   You really should not
   be jumping at all,
   Carmen adds, because

she is Carmen,
responsible.
I won't! Thanks!
I smile real big.
I ain't jumping.
It's for a science project.
To see how things fall.

I'm just happy
you're smiling.
JQ bumps my arm.

What JQ means is I've been distant since my gran went to
the sky. I don't hang out with them as much. I don't laugh
as much. They held my hand at the funeral when a scar
was made in the ground. They used to come over a lot, too,
when Gran was still here, but I never invite them anymore.
I don't want my cousins to see Mama if it's a bad day.

So, we jump on the bus
& head back uptown.
I gotta go to the barbershop
to sweep, get an edge up
& make some pennies.

ROBIN GIBSON: BARBERSHOP

I am almost at the barbershop
when I see Robin Gibson (RG).
He's so cool in his khaki pants,
    white tank top & Chuck Taylors.

He lives in Del Ray,
one block from Grandma Emma's.

    Hey Onyx.
    He gives me a high five.
    You going to the barbershop?

Yea.
I look at his shoes.
I like your shoes.

    Robin puts a quarter
    in my hand.
    Thanks, X.
    See you around.

Robin is like that,
just nice because.

Before Gran went to the sky
    Robin & Willy taught me how
to make a basketball spin
from the free throw line.

Sometimes when I am at Grandma Emma's house,
Robin gathers his friends & all my cousins & we play
2-hand-touch street football with the big kids.
    He always lets us score.

Robin is cool like that.
He reminds me of an astronaut.

DANCY'S BARBERSHOP

The barbershop has one of those things
that looks like a candy cane outside it.

Right beside it is the Black hair salon
with giant things Aunt Julia calls hair dryers,
that look like space helmets to me.

A lot of things
remind me of space—
like when I look at the sky & see stars
or when my basketball goes through a hoop—
    like swish, I think of the planet Saturn.
That has a ring around it like a belt.

    The hair salon door opens.
    X, you better hurry up
    get that nappy hair cut.

Hi, Aunt Julia.
My hair ain't that nappy.
I gotta sweep first.

• • •

Boy, my fingers could get stuck
in that fro. Cut it back for summer.

Aunt Julia goes back into the
salon with the hair dryers
that remind me of space helmets.

EDGE UP

If I sweep up for 2 hours after school,
Mr. Dancy gives me a dollar & a free haircut,
making the edges crisp whenever I need it.

I have to look my best to fly on Tuesday,
so I ask Mr. Dancy for an edge up.

> *Sit down, X,*
> Mr. Dancy says.
> *You ready for summer?*

Yes. Ready for no school,
I say before the men start
talking to each other & not me.

I love the hum of everyone talking.
It feels like a hug, something safe & warm.

The 4 other barbers start talking about
    grown-men things—
    like MLK dying & pay being unfair.
I store all their words in my thought bank.

They talk about things on the ground, though.
I want to ask, *What about space?*
What about God? Where is heaven?

But I don't want to interrupt.
Especially when the older men
playing checkers by the worn magazines
say, *This time 2 years ago the city was burnin'.*

Another man adds,
We peaceful, they shoot us.
We violent, they shoot us.

I think about the superpower
I told RG about.
The boy that could turn bullets
into water.

The professor in the chair
next to me, who really is not
a professor, he just reads a lot, says,
Ya know, if a Black man can make it
from 15 to 35, he has a high chance
of living an entire life.

The barber cutting my hair pats my shoulder.
Alright, X, you stay out of trouble till you're 35.

. . .

I stand.
I will.

In some books, you gotta keep your hair close
because it has wisdom & knowledge in it.
That's what I think about when I am sweeping.

I am gathering knowledge
& even though 35 is a long way
I think I can make it.

I'll learn to fly
& I'll make it.

& Mr. Dancy pays me
enough to buy
a few groceries
for Mama & me.

GROCERIES WITH GRANDMA EMMA

Grandma Emma stops by the barbershop
'cause she needs to pick out some groceries
& she needs help from all of us cousins
to carry them home.

Next, we pass the basketball hoops & get JQ.
Then we stop by the house Carmen is babysitting at.
My other cousins, Willy & Bruno, meet us at the store.

Grandma says,
Go ahead & pick out
your pork chop.

We always buy pork chops for the weekend
during the week because they are cheaper then.
We each get to pick one out & Grandma makes them
with grits, brown gravy & hot buttered rolls
that Aunt Nelly makes & brings over on Saturdays.

Grandma has a big house with 5 bedrooms
on Laverne Avenue. It's the only redbrick house
& it has 2 whole bathrooms. She says,

The house is too quiet with no one in it.

Grandpa went to the sky when I was only 2.
That's why she loves having us all there.

Grandma also picks up bread, eggs, milk & peanut butter
just like my other gran in the sky taught me.
Grandma avoids the aisle with candy in it.
  Willy says, *Grandma,*
  come on, can we just get 1 piece?
  We have money.

  That stuff rots your teeth
  & your brain,
  Grandma says.
We (me, Carmen, JQ, Bruno & Willy)
look at each other knowing
Bruno is going to need his track skills today.

We have another secret mission.
It involves candy.

DINNER & PEACH COBBLER

After we get home & have veggie soup
with homemade rolls on the side, Grandma says,
    Either or. That is what Grandma always says.
You can have a peach or a slice of cobbler.
              Either or.

I always pick the peach,
'cause it takes longer to eat.

Carmen always picks the cobbler,
'cause she likes sweets.

JQ always picks a peach,
'cause he wants to stay in shape.

Willy & Bruno switch all the time
& then Grandma shoos us out of the house
& into the front yard to get some fresh air.

Bruno tightens his shoestrings.

CANDY LAND MISSION

The grocery store with candy is 2 miles away,
but the corner store is only a mile & 1 block
with only 1 squiggly turn.

Bruno is the fastest & Grandma
only looks out the window
to check on us every 30 minutes.

But the sun sets faster
when it's not all the way summer.
So she might call us in early.

You better run fast,
    we say, giving him our pennies.
Bruno takes off almost as fast as the speed of light.
It's a top-secret, get-candy-for-bedtime mission.

CLOSE CALL

Carmen watches the front door
    for Grandma.

I watch the long road
    for Bruno.

Willy & JQ don't watch anything.
    They are ready to distract Grandma
if she comes outside.

I pace, looking down the street at the corner
that Bruno will swing around.

NOTHING.

N O T H I N G.

N O T H I N G.

Grandma calls us once.
    We say, *One second*.

. . .

Grandma calls us twice.
    We say, *Just a minute.*

Then I see Bruno pumping his arms
racing down the street.
    He's coming, I excitedly whisper.

He only has a little farther.

Grandma calls us the third time.
    She is coming to the door.
I said come in!

We whirl around & she looks at Bruno
standing in the middle of the yard & asks,
    Boy, why you breathing so hard?

We just smile,
knowing candy fills Bruno's pockets.

BUNK BED CHATS: FLYING

The taffy sticks to the roof of my mouth.
Y'all think it's easy to get to space?

    Willy is eating a piece of chocolate.
    Yea, it's way up in the sky.

    Carmen adds,
    You would have to be able to fly.

I nod.
Yea.

    What's up with you?
    You been acting weird lately.
    JQ leans over the top bunk
    & looks at me.

I was just thinking.
I shrug.

    Thinking?
    Carmen says,
    licking her fingers.

. . .

Yea, like, we don't know
what's on the moon.

    A bunch of moon stuff, X.
    Bruno laughs.

Nah, I mean what if one of the stones
has some kinda magic, or something.
I try to sound like it's not a big deal.

    Why ya need a special stone?
    JQ asks, leaning over
    the top bunk again.

No reason. Let's just sleep.
I pull the covers over my head.

    X, I miss your gran, too,
    but you know a stone ain't gonna
    bring her back.
    JQ says this to the ceiling,
    to the sky above.

Everyone is real quiet.
Grandma Emma says
the Rüppell's griffon vulture
can fly up to 27,000 feet.

INSTEAD OF GOING TO SCHOOL TUESDAY

I like spending the night at Grandma Emma's
'cause breakfast is always good.
Today Grandma Emma made pancakes.
I eat them quickly & tell Grandma Emma,
    Gotta go, don't wanna be late for school.

& I head home instead of going to school
because it is a good day to try to fly.

I get home & open the door quietly.
I don't hear anything & I know Mama
is sleeping, which happens most of the time now.

I pass the permission slip with the note.
    Mama remembered!
    I take it as a good sign.
I stuff it into my backpack & go to my room.

I strap my wings onto my back
with 2 black belts.
I just gotta believe
real hard.

· · ·

I can fly . . .
    I can fly . . .
        I must fly . . .

We are on the third floor.
The highest I've ever jumped from.

I open my bedroom window.
The mattresses my cousins helped me with
are still stacked perfectly—
    like birthday cakes.

My legs dangle over the side—
    I can fly . . .
        I can fly . . .
            I must fly . . .

BLACK ICARUS (DON'T TRY THIS AT HOME)

I land on my back in the center of the mattress.
The wings on my back crumble like moon dust.

I stare at the sky thinking,
I believed. I believed.
Why can't I fly?
Ain't love magic?

I stand up & cradle my bruised arm.
I leave the wings on the mattress.

It looks like an astronaut with wings
fell from the moon.

I walk up the stairs
back to the apartment
& I climb into my bed,
tuck my knees to my chin
   & become a comet,
      trying to be anywhere but here
but I fell.

I

B

U

R

N

T

O

U

T.

Onyx's Super (Extra) Secret Journal

THE BIG JUMP

I jump buildings
when my cousins & I go exploring.
We climb up on the roof to escape chatter.
I want to fly, I want to jump.
I am only 9 & on top of the roof.
I am bulletproof, nothing can touch me.

I take a deep breath & look up at the sun,
then I run at full speed to jump over
the 3-foot gap. My knee slaps the building,
but I made it.
I flew.
I fly.
I flew.
We fly.

WANING
GIBBOUS
MOON
1970

I look at my back
in the bathroom mirror
& with all my heart
I try to grow them
(wings)
but
nothing.

N
O
T
H
I
N
G.

COOL THING ABOUT SPACE #5

One tiny teaspoon
    of a neutron star
       weighs the same
          as the entire human population.

Heavy.

SCHOOL DAY (9 DAYS TILL SUMMER)

I wear long sleeves to cover my bruised arm.
I take my permission slip with me.
I feel like a stone all day.

This is my last chance. Maybe there is a stone
from the moon at the museum.

On the field trip tomorrow, I'll see if it's there.
    Then, I gotta ask my cousins for help (again).

BOOKSTORE ON 9TH

I take the #9 bus to see Pops a day early
'cause the field trip might take all day.

Pops turns up the music & plays "Tutti Frutti"
& we pretend the bookstore is a stage.

We pretend so hard I think it's real.
It feels like I have an audience.

I stop dancing.
Maybe I didn't believe
    hard enough in flying.

    What's wrong, X?
    Pops touches my shoulder.

I river, I cry like stars
    & I don't know if Pops knows why,
        but he just hugs me & says,
            I know, I know, sometimes things are hard.

· · ·

When my tears dry up, Pops buys me ice cream.
You wanna stay at my place tonight?

I do miss staying at Pops's,
but even if Mama don't remember
if I go or come, I know.

I know I am not leaving her lonely.

Plus, Pops might ask questions
if he sees my bruised arm.

So, I hop on the #9 bus home to Mama
    & to the natural history museum tomorrow.

FRIDAY FIELD TRIP DAY: SMITHSONIAN NATIONAL MUSEUM OF NATURAL HISTORY

I make sure to have 2 waffles in the morning
& I clean off my PF Flyers & I get to the #9
bus stop extra early.

Sister Mary Roberts calls off our names
& we scale the stairs of the bus
& I pretend I am an astronaut
boarding a rocket ship.

It's a bumpy takeoff on the bus.
We jet out of Alexandria
into Washington, DC.

We pass by the Washington Monument,
which looks like a rocket
ready to take off.

The bus parallel parks to let us off
in front of the Smithsonian.

There is a giant elephant guarding
the entrance with his trunk in the air.

Sister Mary Roberts leads us to the space exhibit,
which is past all the dinosaurs.
    Ok, we are here,
    Sister Mary Roberts says.
    Take your time & look around.
I see it. Right away.
It's a rock from space.
I put my hand on the glass & I know
I have to get a tiny part of this rock for Mama.
I have to make sure she doesn't get put away.
        I have to.

    Didn't know you were coming here.
    I look up & Uncle Rob is there.
    It's pretty cool, isn't it?

It's amazing.
It's perfect,
I say.

    I'm getting off soon.
    I can drive you to your grandma's.
    Uncle Rob goes to find Sister Mary Roberts.
I think I nod,
but all I am thinking about
is how to get a piece of that rock.

· · ·

I signed you out with the sisters.
Ready to go to your grandma's?
When I don't answer,
Uncle Rob waves a hand
in front of my face.

Ready! I say.
I am ready to draft
a new plan.

FRONT PORCH CHAT

Uncle Rob drops me off at Grandma Emma's, then goes
inside to talk to her. Me & my cousins sit in a little circle,
like we are the outline of the moon. Like all gravity is
controlled by us & I tell them the plan.

> *Onyx, you telling me you think*
> *this rock is gonna solve everything?*
> JQ throws his arms in the air.

Shhh . . . ,
I whisper.
I had a dream.

> *I dream, too,*
> Carmen huffs.
> *Don't mean I go following them.*

Remember that time 2 years ago
I dreamed Bruno would win States
& it happened,
I whisper.

· · ·

Bruno nods.
He even got the time right.

I ain't saying X don't got a knack
for knowing things, but you
want to break into a museum.
JQ crosses his arms.

The rock is 100 pounds.
We only need a tiny piece,
I say.

How we know it's gonna work?
Carmen puts her hands on her hips.
Rocks ain't magic.

Yes, they are!
My gran said they are!
I ball my fist.
I have to get the rock.

JQ watches me.
Listen, they gotta clean museums.
They leave back doors open for that.

You have to be kidding,
Carmen huffs.
We gonna get arrested.

. . .

Willy shrugs.
If the back door is open,
it ain't really breaking in.

We just accidently walked in,
Bruno adds.

The porch door swings open.
Uncle Rob steps out.
We smile & sit up straight.
What y'all talking about?

Nothing,
I say. *Just about rocks.*

Uncle Rob eyes us for a second.
He tilts his head
like he knows
what we were talking about.
Alright, well, sleep good.

We all say bye,
but we are not
going to sleep good.

Tonight,
we have a mission.
      A heist.

HEIST PREP

Willy sneaks into Grandma Emma's bathroom
& snags the flashlight she keeps under the sink
for when the lights go out during storms.

Carmen looks through our old clothes
that are in the closet (the ones we forget)
& finds everything that is dark blue
or pitch-black for our heist uniforms.

Bruno & JQ distract Grandma Emma
while she is cooking dinner in the kitchen.
They mumble & talk loud over each other
so that I can do my part.

I slip out the house & travel 4 houses down
to where RG stays with his aunt sometimes.
He is on the front porch looking up at the sky.

Hi, RG.
I stand with my hands
behind my back.

. . .

Hey, you staying with
your grandma Emma
tonight? That's nice.

Yup. Hey, I was wondering.
Could you spot me
a dollar?
I look at my feet.

What you need a dollar for?
RG asks, scrunching up his face.

I just . . .
I take a deep breath.
I just . . .

Whoa, whoa.
RG gets out his wallet.
I didn't know you needed
a dollar that bad.

RG hands me the dollar,
the bus fare we need
to save Mama.

I am so happy I run
& hug him hard.

. . .

RG pats my head
& says, *You act like
I just gave you wings!*
& I think he is right.
I feel like I glide back
to Grandma Emma's.

Maybe wings are just
a state of mind.

THE HEIST PLAN

1. Onyx, the Mastermind: Code name X-tra Smart—job is to identify the moon rock, open the case & chip a tiny slither. No one will notice it's gone.
2. Carmen, the Lookout: Code name Doesn't Want a Code Name—job is to stand at the back door & make sure no one is coming.
3. Bruno, the Grabber: Code name Speedy Bro—job is to take the tiny shard of rock & run back to the Metro ahead of everyone.
4. Willy, the Distractor: Code name Willy Wonka—job is to randomly place piles of candies around just to distract people.
5. JQ, the Boss: Code name the *Real* Mastermind—job is to assist where needed, 'cause he is the oldest.

READY SET GO . . .

It's dark & Grandma has turned the TV off.
We get up really quiet
& tie our sheets together
like an endless rope
& slip out the window
into the dark.

The #9 bus is still running
& we pay 20 cents each
to get to the museum.
I use the money
RG gave me.

We bounce up & down
leaving Alexandria behind
& crossing the magical line
into Washington, DC.

We get off at the Smithsonian stop
& walk up the long Mall to the museum.
We stay extra quiet when we see the back door is open.

. . .

Wide open, like the door was waiting for us.

JQ stops.
Why this feel like a trap?

Feels like a setup,
Bruno whispers.

READY SET ... OH NO!

I take a step toward the door & a bell starts ringing.
Not like an alarm bell, almost like a Christmas ornament
    bell.

   What is that?
   Carmen says, hiding behind JQ.
The Christmas bell stops
& Pops & Uncle Rob
step out.

You kids have a lot
of explaining to do.
Pops looks down at us.

That's when we know we are caught.
Uncle Rob must've heard
our super-secret plan
when I asked for help on the porch.

He must've told Pops.
He ruined it all.

Onyx's Super (Extra) Secret Journal

(I FAILED)

NOW WHAT WILL HAPPEN TO MAMA?
NOW WHAT WILL HAPPEN TO MAMA?
NOW WHAT WILL HAPPEN TO MAMA?
NOW WHAT WILL HAPPEN TO MAMA?
NOW WHAT WILL HAPPEN TO MAMA?
NOW WHAT WILL HAPPEN TO MAMA?
NOW WHAT WILL HAPPEN TO MAMA?
NOW WHAT WILL HAPPEN TO MAMA?
NOW WHAT WILL HAPPEN TO MAMA?
NOW WHAT WILL HAPPEN TO MAMA?

THIRD
QUARTER
MOON
1970

I can't get the rock.
I can't get to space.
I can't.
I can't.

THE TRUTH FAMILY

Each of us gets dropped off at home. Then Pops pulls up
outside of Grandma's 2-story redbrick house & I start
crying stars & tell him the truth. I tell him Mama misplaces
her memories & it has gotten worse with Gran gone. I tell
him I tried to fly & that I didn't try hard enough. I tell him
I need a piece of that rock to get Mama's memories back,
but I failed again.

Pops doesn't yell.
He gathers me in his arms
& lets me cry.

He holds me at arm's length.
You did not fail at anything, X.

But in my dream Gran said,
Onyx, you just gotta fly.
You gotta soar as high up as you can.
Onyx, you gotta be strong like your stones.
Remember, there is a stone for every situation.

You have got some imagination, X.
Pops smiles. *I think what your gran meant*

was, use your family,
your community.
Together things can be less heavy.

What's that mean?
I sniffle.

It means together.
We can figure this out together.
Pops gives me a hug.

Pops looks me in the eyes.
Together we will build wings.
Together we will fly & figure this out.

& for a moment I don't think
flying has anything to do with
leaving the ground.

It's how your heart feels
& mine feels lifted
& held & soaring.

FAMILY TO THE RESCUE

The next morning Grandma Emma & Pops
come with me to see Mama.

I unlock the door for them
& we shuffle into the small apartment.

Dishes are in the sink,
    a TV hums
       & there is a pot filled
       with old food on the stove.

I walk back to Mama's room to wake her up.
I open her door slowly, so she won't be startled,
but she is not there.

I run to my room.
She is not there either.

I run to the family room.
Mama is Gone!

WHERE IN ALEXANDRIA IS MAMA?

Grandma, Pops & me race down to the car.
My heart keeps hopping into my throat
like a frog.

Onyx, where would your mama go?
Grandma asks in a soft voice.

I dunno.
I wipe tears from my eyes.

Listen, Onyx, you know.
You just have to think.
Pops looks me in the eyes.

I think as hard as I can.
I try to get ancestors, Gran,
anyone to tell me.

I think of all the adventures
Mama & me went on,
    then it hits me,

like an asteroid—
Mama's at Gran's grave.

'Cause I know my mama.

MAMA & GRAN

When we get to the cemetery
    I can already see Mama.
She only has her robe & slippers on.
She sits on her knees in the grass
tracing Gran's name in the stone.

Mama.
I sit down beside her.
Pops & my other grandma stay back.

    Hi, Honey.
    Mama has tears in her eyes.

Mama,
it's ok.
I hold her hand.
She squeezes it.

    X, you know what I forgot?
    Mama rocks back & forth.
    I forgot my mama died.

. . .

I grab Mama's other hand.
I try to be like gravity.
I try to make her steady.

> *X, I think we are going to need*
> *a little bit of help.*
> Mama kisses the top of my head.

We got lots of people to help,
I say. *Family & neighbors.*

> *Tell me that poem again, Honey.*
> *The one about a funeral.*
> Mama looks at me
> like I am the sun.

I repeat the poem I wrote.
A funeral is when a scar
is cut in the ground
& a box is lowered
into the scar
& then all the dirt
is pushed back
but the ground
always remembers
that someone
opened it.

· · ·

So it stitches
back
different.

> *Our family is gonna stitch back different.*
> Mama turns & hugs me.
> *But we are going to be alright.*

DAYS LATER: THE DOCTORS SAY

Grandma Emma & Pops take Mama to the hospital
for tests while I go to school,
smiling a bit more in the lunchroom again.
& Pops says he will talk to the wellness-check person.

We have been staying with Grandma Emma
in her big brick house that is lonely for her.

The doctor says Mama has dementia,
which means a lot of things,
but mostly that her memories
sometimes turn into black holes.

Routine helps,
but change can make it worse.

The doctor thinks that is what happened
after my gran (in the sky) passed.

Everyone on Grandma Emma's street knows Mama now
& if they see her outside without Grandma they call.

THE BIG CHOICE

When I walk in from school
Grandma Emma & Mama are sitting
waiting for me & I wonder
if I have done something wrong.

> *X, we have 2 questions for you,*
> Mama starts. *First, do you want*
> *to go to public school with your cousins?*

I drop my backpack.
Yes!

> *Second, do you & your mama*
> *want to live here, with me?*
> Grandma Emma smiles a big smile.

Grandma Emma puts on
"Ain't No Mountain High Enough"
    & we dance,
'cause Gran (in the sky) always said,

If you are too happy to speak or cry,
you can always dance.

So, we dance
like glittering flying stars
& we smile as full as the moon.

WANING
CRESCENT
MOON
1970

Looks like a sly grin

like a bowl waiting to be filled
with stars
but mostly like
a griffin wing.

SUMMERTIME IN THE CITY

It's the last day of school.
    Next year I'll go to public school
& I can't wait to be in the same school as my cousins.
Pops & Grandma Emma & Mama met with the social
    worker
& ironed everything out smooth.

I can't wait times 10 for summertime
when they open the fire hydrants on our street
& the water floods & when I think hard enough—
    it's an ocean with sea turtles as round as the moon.

Summertime is for hot dogs & fireworks.
For Bruno racing to get candy
& only sometimes getting caught.

Carmen, JQ, Bruno & Willy meet me at our corner
    & we race toward Grandma's because we are having
a first day of summer sleepover.

I am going to beat all of you,
Bruno says, surging ahead.

I run fast, too,
faster than lightning
that zigzags through the sky.

ONYX & BEYOND

My gran (in the sky)
must have bargained
with heaven & said,
 Let the boy fly.
'Cause I swear in my shadow
I see them again,
my griffin boy wings.

We grew them back.
I can fly.
I can do anything.
 With my pops
 with my mama
  with my cousins
  with my gran (in the sky)
   with my grandma Emma (on Earth)
    with RG (believing in me)
    with my community.
     Together we soar: magic.

NEW MOON
AGAIN

In Loving Memory of Robin Gibson
(1951–1970)

AUTHOR'S NOTE

Although Onyx Armstrong is a fictional character, he is largely crafted from stories that my dad, Mario McBride, told me about growing up in Alexandria in the 60s and 70s. My dad, like everyone in his family, is a storyteller and when my sister and I were young, he told us countless bedtime stories about city life and the #9 bus into DC.

My dad told us about jumping out of third-story windows onto old mattresses and sprinting to the corner store for candy. He told us about Robin Gibson and how all the young kids looked up to him and played street football. When the film *Remember the Titans* came out, my dad was invited to the premiere and was able to point out all the historical inaccuracies, because he lived it.

My dad and I originally set out to write this book together, but he found he preferred telling stories and having me pull out the essence in them. So, that's what we did. My dad wrote a few poems ("When Mama Remembers," "Day & Night") and told me hundreds of stories, and I crafted a story with heart, hope, and (like always) a little bit of magic.

In this book, Onyx's mama has progressive dementia—a condition my dad's mom now has. To put it simply, dementia is a condition that about 3 million people are diagnosed with every year. It impairs your memory & your judgment. There is no cure for dementia and it can often get worse with time.

Everyone knows Martin Luther King Jr., but not everyone knows about Robin Gibson. In Alexandria and DC, his death was a big deal. He was a real person who was shot and killed at the 7-Eleven on Glebe Road on May 29, 1970, for allegedly stealing razor blades from the store. He was only 19 years old. His life was taken far too early. More information on Robin Gibson can be found here: nytimes.com/1970/06/07/archives/weeks-disorders-end-in-alexandria.html.

Robin Gibson (source: *Alexandria Gazette*)

My dad, Mario McBride, wants you to know that you should take the time to be a kid and don't grow up too fast. Take your time and grow into your wings. He also says, *Don't forget to stay a kid for the rest of your life.*

POEMS BY MARIO McBRIDE

DAY & NIGHT

Watching the pole vault at a high school track meet
reminds me of my mama,
she switches up day & night.

So, day pole-vaults over night
& Mama is caught up
in a never-ending fight,
she starts her walkabout into
    twilight
       as day
           pole-vaults over night.

WHEN MAMA REMEMBERS

Talk to her all night long
when she remembers how
she used to cut worms in half
& pretend she had wings
as a kid, just like me.

'Cause this disease
is genuine.

I can't go backward
so I love Mama in the present.

Thank you for reading this Feiwel & Friends book.
The friends who made *Onyx & Beyond* possible are:

Jean Feiwel, Publisher

Liz Szabla, VP, Associate Publisher

Rich Deas, Senior Creative Director

Anna Roberto, Executive Editor

Holly West, Senior Editor

Kat Brzozowski, Senior Editor

Dawn Ryan, Executive Managing Editor

Raymond Ernesto Colón, Director of Production

Foyinsi Adegbonmire, Editor

Rachel Diebel, Editor

Emily Settle, Editor

Brittany Groves, Assistant Editor

Michelle McMillian, Designer

Lelia Mander, Production Editor

Follow us on Facebook or visit us online at mackids.com.
Our books are friends for life.